BLOODY MARY

Gentle Woman

BLOODY MARY

Gentle Woman

Frances Grace Reinehr

Foundation Books
Lincoln, Nebraska

 For information address Foundation Books, Inc., P. O. Box 29229, Lincoln, NE 68529.

5 4 3 2 1

Library of Congress Cataloging-in-Publication Data

Reinehr, Frances Grace, 1934-
Bloody Mary : gentle woman / Frances Grace Reinehr.
p. cm.
1. Partington, Mary Ann, 1889-1979. 2. Lincoln Region (Neb.)--Biography. 3. Teachers--Nebraska--Lincoln Region--Crimes against. 5. Vandalism--Nebraska--Lincoln Region. I. Title.
CT275.P3876R45 1989
978.2'293--dc20
[B]

89-84199
CIP

ISBN 0-934988-16-1 (pbk)

Cover Photo: Mary Ann Partington, 1976. Photograph by Nancy Davis Richardson.

Aunt Mary
simply refused to dwell on the tragic
aspects of life.

-- Mary Ann Kellogg Davis

Contents

Illustrations

Preface

In 1974 a wide-eyed child in my fifth grade class at Elliott School in Lincoln, Nebraska, first introduced me to the story of Bloody Mary. This child had just had a terrifying encounter with a "witch woman" who lived in a haunted house north of the city, guarded by a herd of fierce goats.

"Tell me more," I said. "I want to know exactly what happened."

"The other night," she said breathlessly, "Mama and us kids was driving on North 27th down there by Payless Shoes and there she was walking. Mama said, 'Look! There's Mary Partington, that old Bloody Mary. She'd like a ride home.'

"We cried and begged Mama not to let her in the car, but Mama stopped and put her in the front seat. Us kids stayed in the back and didn't say one word. Mama took her way out north in the country and then Bloody Mary said, 'You can let me out here.'

"We watched Mary walk up the long lane to that farmhouse. It looked like a movie set. I don't think she wanted us to see in her house. It was haunted."

Intrigued by this story, I began to collect more stories about Mary Partington and to share them with my students.

In 1985 "Bloody Mary's House" appeared in *Ghosts of Lincoln* by Stephen Boyd. My students wanted to know if that story was about "our" Mary. How could they learn more?

Those students and I began a class research project. We collected newspaper accounts of Mary, visited with Partington family members, visited the knoll on 44th and Superior once crowned by Mary's rambling farmhouse. There she had endured siege from generations of teenagers intent on a rite of passage.

When the students and I arrived at the home of Mary's relatives on our first visit, I was struck by the formality. The family was dressed up and seated us as special guests much as my own Irish family would have done. I was surprised because the name Partington sounded English to me. It was, but the other side of the family was Irish. They told us tales of their Irish great-grandmother, Ella Rhatigan, whose roots reached back to Dublin to a time when storytellers were respected like landowners.

The students were off and running on their research project. They went on their own to

Calvary Cemetery and found Mary's grave. Afterwards they burst into the classroom with the news and pictures. "We've been there! See? Here's her actual grave!"

A neighbor of Mary's for over thirty years talked to us at Davey, Nebraska.

We wrote down those experiences and the children spoke of the day their stories about Mary would be published.

As those students went on into high school, I went on collecting--pursuing the legend of Bloody Mary and enjoying the search with a new generation of students. Our questions continued: "What happened in Mary's life to earn her the title 'Bloody Mary'? What was her story?

Now those questions can be answered. With this book the dream of my students is being fulfilled. Those who brought me the first stories can read what they and others have discovered about Mary Partington whom some called "Bloody Mary."

Frances Grace Reinehr
Lincoln, Nebraska
February, 1989

Acknowledgments

First of all, my thanks to Mary herself. She told some of her life story in *The Partington Family: Early Days in the United States*, which she gave to her family as a Christmas gift in 1976. She also wrote a number of autobiographical stories for her niece, Mary Ann Kellogg Davis. Parts of these stories are included here. Her nephew, Lee Partington, and his wife, Carol, supplied many stories about their Aunt Mary. Their children, James, John, Mary Catherine, and Peggy, also remembered their great aunt. Mabel Knox, Mary's sister, recalled early days of her pioneer family. Mary's nephew, John Kellogg, told me about his Aunt Mary and what she meant to him and his family. Her niece, Mary Ann Kellogg Davis, tape recorded several hours of recollections about her memorable Aunt Mary for me.

Members of the Lancaster County Sheriff's Department who knew and remembered Mary filled in gaps. Former Nebraska Attorney visit to the scene of the killing. Judge William Blue supplied his perceptions and remembrances as a deputy county attorney. Lincoln police officers willingly told me of their encounters. Historians, newspaper reporters, fire inspectors, archivists in Wyoming and Nebraska supplied records to me. The *Lincoln Star*, *Lincoln Journal* and *Lincoln Sunday Journal-Star* newspapers granted me permission to use their photographs.

Initial co-researchers, 5th and 6th grade students in my storywriting/composition class, 1985:

Amy Anderson
Bobby Anderson
Donnie Bourne
Melanie Burger
Nicole Bush
Denise Dickinson
Ronnie Ederington
Broady Fuller
Tracy Hallquist
Shelly Justvig
Tara Kringel
Damon Lee
Jeff Maldavs
Petrina Martinez
Sung Park
Eric Peterson
Dixie Piepho
Michelle Polk
Stephanie Range
Cynthia Strand
Michelle Wade

Mike Anderson
Mike Atkins
Jennifer Aupperle
Shayne Bennett
Gene Brandl
Jennifer Davis
Scott Delgado
Mike Doetkott
Olga Garmiris
Jason Glather
Melissa Johnson
Shannon Kern
Bridget Liming
Loren Lutton
Jennifer Mateer
Michelle Muhs
Chris Range
Nicole Rezac
Jeff Ridenour
Tiffany Ruzanic

I offer my gratitude to all those who helped me realize one does not write alone, especially Stephen K. Hutchinson, my persistent editor, who believed in me and kept encouraging me through questions to help me find the story behind the legend.

1.
I Got One But It Didn't Help

In the early hours of Wednesday, October 26, 1966, Mary Partington huddled under the blankets and tried not to hear the noise of a prowler in her lonely farmhouse north of Lincoln, Nebraska. Seventy-seven years old, she had slept in this bedroom for forty years. The first twenty had been peaceful, but now vandals had been breaking her windows, painting obscene words on the side of her house, and even attacking her. Someone had gotten in and tied her with rope.

Who had come to torment her now? The noises persisted. Why didn't the sheriff come? She had called nearly an hour ago. No sirens. Now a thud on the side of the house. Breaking glass!

Mary bolted upright, grabbed her wire rimmed glasses off the bedside table. The floor felt cold. She stepped into black high topped shoes, grabbed her 12 gauge Meriden Firearms single shot. She'd loaded it with #6 shot that came in those blue plastic casings. This should be enough to scare them. Her flashlight in one hand, shotgun in the other, she crept downstairs.

When Mary entered her dark kitchen, she saw the head of a person silhouetted in the large broken pane of the shadeless window.

Mary aimed and fired. The figure dropped away. She turned around, believing she'd frightened the intruder away, leaned the shotgun into the corner and dialed the sheriff's office again.

When the sheriff's office heard Mary's first call that morning, the officers assigned to her area were a mile north and three miles west of Centerville, Nebraska--a long way from the Partington farmstead on 44th and Superior. The sheriff's department turned to the Lincoln Police, even though Mary's place was not yet in the city. The police were familiar enough with Mary's vandalism problems. Breaking and entry had happened again and again. The old woman shouldn't be living alone; now she was developing into a legend. It wasn't only the harassments; the kids seemed to make it a rite of passage to go out and rile her. Crazy old woman in a house out of the early 1900's.

Lincoln police officer Lt. Satterwaite who arrived at Mary's house first said, "I went to the front door because I grew up in the area and had seen Mary many times at Green's service station. I felt I sort of knew her. Actually, she was well known to all in law enforcement because of the stories and rumors that circulated about her.

"Mary was nervous and scared like anyone would have been, but she was not hysterical when we arrived.

"Mary had been victim of dare games and double dare games for years. The dare was simply to sneak up to her house and steal some item, even a shingle, without her hearing you. The double dare included walking down 44th street in the dark to Pigman's, a fellow down the road about a mile. With Salt Creek in the vicinity, many of us worried that there would be a drowning out there someday.

"We sealed off the area because, when we arrived, we found a man lying straight back, his feet next to a crock jar he'd apparently stood on to look into the house. Maybe he had been window peeking. The reason for his being there was silenced when Mary hit him in the face with gunshot. He had a hole in his right cheek and had died instantly.

"I remember there was a large, full moon the night of the shooting so the victim would have been well silhouetted in the brightness of the night.

"Once members of the sheriff's department, and Paul Douglas and William Blue from the County Attorney's office, had arrived, those of us from the Police Department left."

William Blue, the Chief Deputy County Attorney, described it this way:

"I remember Sheriff Karnopp and I getting out of our car and walking to the front door. It was extremely dark. The house seemed dark, even though it was lit with kerosene lamps.

"Mary greeted us at the door. She said to Sheriff Karnopp, 'See, you told me if I got a phone that would help solve this problem. I got one, but it didn't help.'"

Mary had resisted electricity and plumbing, and had preferred living in her isolated rural setting.

Blue continued: "When I got to Mary's house, it was as though I stepped out of one era and entered another, because her home was furnished with antiques and kerosene lamps.

"I was called to accompany Sheriff Karnopp to investigate the possibility of a homicide, but Mary was never charged."

Paul Douglas, Lancaster County Attorney, remembered the evening well. "Sheriff Karnopp and I went out there to investigate the reported shooting. The kitchen was quite dark so I used my flashlight to look around. There was glass lying on the sink and the floor so it appeared the window had been broken from the outside

"Mary was her usual self. By that I mean she was no raving maniac. A direct woman, Mary told Karnopp and me about what had happened:

"Mary said, 'I had been upstairs in my bedroom waiting for the sheriff because I had called them earlier when I heard prowling noises. When I heard glass breaking, I got up and came downstairs, carrying my shotgun which I keep beside my bed.

"'When I reached the first floor, I put my gun next to the door casing near the telephone and called the sheriff's office. When I hung up the phone, I heard more glass breaking and I saw someone in the west window of the kitchen. So, I picked up my shotgun, and a voice said, "We will fight!"

"'I didn't know what to do. I thought he was by the sink in the house. I was frightened and I pulled the trigger. He disappeared so I called the sheriff's department again.'"

Earl Eldon Hill, the man who came to Mary's looking for some unknown reason found death. He came in a 1960 blue Ford Fairlane and left in a Roper's Mortuary hearse heading for St. Elizabeth's Hospital and an autopsy.

Officers checked the Fairlane to see if Hill had run out of gas. There was gas, but no keys. In fact, they never did find the Fairlane ignition keys.

Sheriff Karnopp phoned Mary's nephew, Lee Partington, to come be with Mary. When the officers left that night, they took Mary's shotgun with them.

Lee recalled, "I went to Aunt Mary's because my dad was ill and couldn't go. My dad, James, was Mary's brother. They were very close and he often stopped in at Mary's.

"We were upset when we got the call that somebody had been shot out at Mary's. I went right out. For several years we'd been trying to get Mary to move into town. But she would have nothing to do with the idea, even though she couldn't take care of the house very well any more. She was seventy-seven, but Mary was independent, self-sufficient and didn't like others to make her decisions.

"I remember her so well that night, sitting there all hunched over. I asked her if she would come home with me a few days. She straightened up, looked at me through those wire-rimmed glasses and said, 'You have things to do and I have things to do. You can go on home.'"

When Mrs. Virginia Hill came to Lincoln to claim the personal belongings of her son, Earl, the eighth child in a family of twelve, she related some of his history. "We were farm parents. Earl had a normal life through grammar school, but all my children knew a father who allowed them no luxuries, only life's necessities. Eldon wanted to participate in 4-H so he could compete in livestock raising, but this was not allowed by his father.

"My son was quiet, well-mannered, but extremely shy about girls. Eldon and his recent girl friend had separated three times the last year.

"A year after he graduated from high schcol, Eldon ran away from home and attempted to join the service, but he had begun to experience mental problems. About 1961 Eldon moved to Lincoln where he lived with the brother of his girl friend. The relationship with his girl friend developed into problems. A few days before the shooting, his roommate said Eldon was a man in a haze. Two days before that night, he had been to a minister to discuss his problems."

Earl Eldon Hill did work for a Lincoln construction firm, but he had been in and out of St. Elizabeth's Mental Health Center several times. Three times he had been a mental patient at the state hospital in Clarinda, Iowa.

Several days after the death of Hill, Paul Douglas announced there would be "no criminal charges filed in connection with the shotgun slaying of the former Iowa mental patient, Earl Eldon Hill." Douglas said later, in an interview, "The event was clearly justifiable homicide. The guy was breaking and entering. Mary clearly had the right to defend herself."

But the title, "Bloody Mary," now took on new meaning for hundreds of young imaginations. The teasing and taunting continued and the thrill increased.

Mary lived eleven more years on the farm in the firm belief she had the right to live her life as she chose, in her home.

Fig. 1. Earl Eldon Hill's senior class photo taken from his high school yearbook, Villisca, IA, 1956. The caption in the yearbook said, "ELDON HILL 'I'll only speak when spoken to.' Football 2-3; Track 2; FFA 2; Letter Club 1; Basketball 1; Hi-Y 2." Photograph by Woltz Studio, Des Moines, IA.

Fig. 2. View of the southwest corner of Mary Ann Partington's house, 44th and Superior Streets, Lincoln, NE. Photographed and used with a newspaper article on the Earl Eldon Hill shooting (*Lincoln Star*, October 27, 1966). Reprinted, by permission, from Lincoln Journal-Star, Lincoln, NE.

2.
Sunshine and Fair Weather

Born in Lincoln, Nebraska, March 22, 1889, Mary Ann Partington came as the first child of Harold James and Ella (Rhatigan) Partington. Lincoln, a frontier prairie capital in a state only twenty-two years old, had fresh memories of horse-drawn streetcars, of financial panics and grasshopper attacks. Ben Harrison was spending his first month as twenty-third president of the United States.

Mary's father at twenty-one had left his Heywood, England, home only four years earlier, made his way to a port and climbed into the steerage section of an America-bound ship.

Harold had left his widowed mother, Ann Tomlinson Partington, and his sisters, Mary Alice, Annie and Lydia, in the charge of his uncles. Of the four brothers, Richard, Harold, Joseph and Charles, the latter is noted in family history as taking particular care of the women. Harold's mother, by the way, had once earned first prize at a Queen Victoria dairy event. The award, a sterling silver tea set, remains in the Partington family, passing to the first son of each generation.

Harold landed in Lincoln short of money. His English experience in dairying helped him land a job with dairyman Rolifson. After two years cleaning barns, milking cows and suffering a daily fare of molasses with his board and room, he went to work for Abbott's Dairy.

While boarding and rooming with the Alonzo Abbotts, a redheaded Irish lass came to work as cook, housekeeper and companion to Mrs. Abbott. Ella Rhatigan took notice of the dark-haired Harold with his English accent. Harold appreciated the girl with the hearty laugh and the starched, box pleated skirts.

Ella had been born in Bernard, Iowa, the same year Harold was born in England. She was the seventh child in a family of eight. Trained at St. Mary's Academy in Dubuque, Iowa, Ella came to Nebraska to teach in McCook, then after a year had come to the Lincoln Hotel as a waitress and seamstress. Mrs. Abbott had met her there while living at the hotel a few months, cooling off from a family quarrel.

Ella and Harold married October 21, 1887 and moved to G Street near the southern edge of Lincoln. At the time, cows grazed on the University of Nebraska campus.

Soon Harold went to work for "Pa Mills," another dairyman, but Ella and Harold

Fig. 3. Wedding portrait of Harold Partington and Ella Rhatigan Partington taken in 1887. Photograph from the collection of Lee and Carol Partington. Photographer unknown.

Fig. 4. Studio portrait of Mary Ann Partington taken in 1896. Photograph from the collection of Lee and Carol Partington. Photograph by Elite Studio, Lincoln, NE.

continued a strong bond of friendship with the Abbott family.

One day Abbott came to visit Harold and Ella to say he was retiring from the farm and offered them to rent his farm and take over the dairy business.

Mary Ann, named for Ella's mother, was six weeks old when her parents took her in a clothes basket to the Abbott farm north of Lincoln. Between 1889 and 1904, Ella bore eight more children: James Harold, Ada E., Hazel, Anna E., Charles R., Mabel, Joe and Grace.

Many years later, Mary described the Abbott house: "It was quite new. There were three rooms upstairs and three rooms downstairs. There was a coal bin, windmill, pump, cow barns, a hay rack, a plow, two horses and four or five cows. (The Partingtons obviously hadn't continued the dairy production the Abbotts had.) All water was carried from the pump at the windmill and coal was the fuel burned for cooking and heating. There were usually two hired men earning thirty dollars a month plus board and room. Extra men were hired at harvest time."

Harold raised a few acres of corn, but primarily harvested the prairie hay on the expansive riverbottom pastures. The family gardened to set the table.

Ella Partington became famous for her A-1 bread, cakes, pies and doughnuts. She washed on a scrubboard and ironed with a flatiron heated on the kitchen range. Neighbors remembered her as a beautiful, capable woman of strong religious convictions. She invited the mission priest from St. Patrick's in the nearby town of Havelock into her home to say masses. She became St. Patrick's altar society president.

Mary recalled in her 1975 family history how her father "usually took a break from his rigorous schedule on Saturday evenings when he walked into Havelock, a railroad community south and east of the place where he and his family lived. He went in to get a shave and buy a roast for Sunday's dinner.

"Our family had parties occasionally. We went to Church and we all played musical instruments. We girls made our own clothing, but our brothers had tailor mades. My word! The ironing! We wore two full petticoats. We ironed everything but the baby's (diapers). The wind did that."

When each Partington child turned five, he or she began walking to the wooden framed school in University Place, another community about a mile south of the Partington home. Later they walked to the University, four miles farther. In severe weather Harold did hitch up horse and buggy to take the children.

Mary, James, Ada and Anna finished high school at University Place's Wesleyan Academy, while Hazel completed high school in the new University High School opened in 1913. The first University Place annual, the Cub, mentions a sophomore party at the Partingtons when "Seniors in search of refreshments raided the party. Nothing was harmed but the carpet."

When the frost came out of the ground in the spring, the road to the Partingtons ran hub-deep mud. Kids walking home from school took off shoes and waded through the slop.

But, with spring, came the greening of the hay meadows. In summer the men drove the horse-drawn mowers, hay sweeps and stacker. They "laid by" the corn in July with the last cultivating before the corn grew too tall.

"Sunshine and fair weather," Mary wrote, "made green fragrant hay. Fog, dew and rain made the help sing 'More rain and more rest, us boys like that the best.' And they played cards in the corn crib while Mama cooked dinner and supper and us kids washed dishes, carried cobs and chips and drew a bucket of water from the well.

"Hay making meant making lunches for the men. We had a big clothes basket cleanly lined with paper and into it went homemade bread sandwiches, filled with tender boiled beef or ham. Sometimes there were boiled eggs, but nothing messy. But there were always pies, usually two pies so pieces were big. I remember the hot one from the oven that Papa cut with the axe. He then removed his shoe and put his piece on the sole of his shoe to eat as soon as it cooled. Shoe soles in the hay field are smooth and clean as a new pin.

"The water taken to the field was drinking water. Us kids took the men's lunches and water to the field in the buggy pulled by 'Old Bird.' We also took tin cups and the big jug of hot coffee with cream and sugar made by

Mama in the kitchen. The men ate their dinner in the shade under the wagon.

"The men watered the horses from a barrel of water loaded up in the morning and covered with gunny sacks to keep it cool. We kids were not allowed to come to the field for a drink of water unless we were working there. Keg water was for the workers.

"Papa always did the stacking. He would build a twelve to sixteen ton stack of hay straight as his barn. No hay stack ever fell over. Once a rattlesnake was dumped from the stacker and Papa threw it off with the pitchfork."

In 1906, the Partington family moved into their new home at 44th and Superior about a mile north of the old Abbott place.

3.
If You Start a Fire, Put It Out

The Partingtons chose a knoll nine rods east of Salt Creek for their new twelve-room home. Neighbors referred to this house in the Atkinson Division as the marvel of the community. While two and three bedroom farmhouses were common, the Partingtons built six bedrooms, two parlors, and carpeted them with rich red. The carpet set off the brand new piano and the Victorian furniture.

Harold insisted on a recreation room which ran the width of the house on the second floor. He said the pool table in there would keep his children from going to the pool halls in Havelock.

The windmill pumped water to a tank in the wash house and also into a 3,000 gallon storage tank which supplied water to a sink in the kitchen and to the bathtub upstairs. Water lines also ran to the barns. A float inside the water tank enabled them to see from the outside if the tank was getting low. They never drained it except for occasional scrubbings. A built-in hopper-bottomed self-feeding coal bin supplied fuel for the kitchen range and hot water tank. A sanitary drain led out to a lake west of the horse barn. No longer did Partington children have to carry coal or water on wash day, or throw the soapy water from dishes on the petunia beds.

Harold, in later years, described nearby Salt Creek as "much wider and cleaner with chokecherry bushes and wild plum trees bordering the edges."

However, Salt Creek flooded nearly every spring. One spring the Larson's barn and granary on the west side of the creek floated downstream, breaking up on a couple of curves. Another neighbor, Brethower, who had a half dozen of his cows at Larsons, tried to drive them home and drowned in the attempt. They found his corpse north of Partingtons the next day.

That death and other flooding problems brought about the straightening of Salt Creek.

"The Partington Pond," recalled neighbor Orville Smith, "was full of carp and bullheads in the summer and it froze in the winter, drawing many young people from Havelock and Lincoln to ice skating parties. Mr. Partington was fond of young people and established only one rule for the skaters who came together to skate, sing, laugh, toast wieners and marshmallows, and to thaw out iced mittens and numbing toes: 'If you start a fire, put it out.' Mr. Partington was a hayman so fire was an enemy if it got away.

"One time four of us decided to skate down Salt Creek from the Partington Pond to Waverly (almost six miles). It was New Year's Eve and the New Year's Eve skating party had become quite a big affair for many of us. Well, four of us started out and skated all the way . . . Back in those days Salt Creek wound around back of Partington's and there were also many small lakes . . . It was one great night."

In 1908 Harold and Ella took their youngest, four-year-old Grace, to England. They hired a guardian, Lettie Swanson, for child care.

Mary who by this time was twenty recalled: "We thought Lettie was ancient. Oh, we were respectful enough, but the young folks swarmed into our Valhalla on Sundays. One time we wired up Lettie's pony's tail. She was distraught and when the boys finally undid the damage, she was filled with happiness. I remember Lettie cried when Mama and Papa returned home."

Then there were the porch parties. The wrap-around front porch facing the south provided the family with a view of the growing city of Lincoln. Mabel recalled, "We used to sit on the porch and watch the construction of the Capitol building. On the Fourth of July we were able to watch the fireworks displays at

Burlington Beach, now Capitol Beach. We enjoyed one of the best views around because in those days there were few buildings to obstruct our vision."

Fig. 5. View of southwest side of the Partington house looking across the Partington Pond. The pond was formerly known as Creighton Lake, after the previous owner Charles F. Creighton. Photograph taken between 1915 and 1920. Photograph from the collection of Lee and Carol Partington. Photographer unknown.

4.
I'm Not Going to Have Any Trouble

Mary Ann Partington, perhaps because of her experience as the oldest of a brood of eight, chose a teaching career. "She developed an air of authority," Mabel recalled. "I remember when she had to come after us children who had wandered into the woods. She marched us all back carrying a switch, but she didn't need the switch."

After Mary passed the examination for a teaching certificate she, at the age of twenty-one, signed a contract for $320 to teach fourteen boys and eight girls for 160 days in District #134, Waverly. The next school term, 1911-1912, Mary taught in District #86 nearer home next to Havelock (Norwood Park). This contract included one more pupil, eighteen more days and $405 for the term. Now she walked most days, or drove a horse and buggy. Neola Studnicka recalled "watching Mary drive by . . . how wonderful she looked."

In 1915 after visiting an aunt and uncle in St. Paul, Minnesota, Mary took a teaching job in Max, Minnesota, in the woods only a hundred miles from Canada.

Mary wrote of this later: "I found a placement for $60 per month where the former teacher refused to teach. On March 1st, 1915, I took a train to Bena where we had to find . . . a sleigh ride across the frozen Lake Winnibigoshish to Max. The ride was a cold one, so cold I could not open my pocketbook for the five dollars to pay the driver. He helped me.

"When I arrived in Max, I was to call the County Superintendent for acceptance. He said, 'If you have any trouble, let me know.'

"I answered him, 'I'm not going to have any trouble.'

"'Oh,' he said, 'Oh, aren't you?'

"I simply answered, 'No.'

"I found a board and room placement at twelve dollars a month and I was happy. The former teacher's trouble was chiefly religious. She was English, Irish and Episcopalian. Wow! I was English, Irish, and, worse yet, Catholic, but there I was, thirty-five miles from Bena.

"I never did have any trouble with my scholars, nor their parents, nor any of the neighbors.

"I left Max in June via St. Paul, stopping for a short visit with my relatives. Life in Max was simple. We had no cars and we walked wherever we went. Mr. Loomis used to bring my lunch to the school one-fourth mile distant from the cabin. I think this was my greatest experience. I was asked to remain for the coming year, but I returned home to go to college. Great people they were, honest, simple and kind."

Mary returned to the farm and put herself through the University of Nebraska on the money she had saved. On May 27, 1918, she received her B.A. with a major in English and a Teachers' College Diploma and University Teacher Certificate. Her courses had included Rhetoric, German, English Literature, Advanced Composition, Nineteenth Century English History, sciences and teacher training courses. Then followed a year of teaching Junior High at Lewiston, Nebraska, and teaching of chemistry and other sciences in Genoa, Nebraska, along with her sister, Hazel, who taught eighth grade English.

"How different the two women appeared," recalled a Genoa student. "Hazel was bubbly and feminine, usually dressed in suits with frilly white blouses. Mary was tall and heavy with a definite air of authority. She usually dressed in black taffeta, but I remember once when she wore a purple woolen dress, some chemicals dripped on her garment leaving holes. Mary showed no outward concern about this.

"Also Hazel and her friends left the boarding house to go to dances, but Mary stayed home."

Mary went with her sister to teach in other school districts, but in 1920, Mary went to Moorcroft, Wyoming. The small community on the Belle Fourche River in Crook County did not hold her long. The following fall she moved to Ogallala, Nebraska, to teach.

In 1922, with her mother's deteriorating health, Mary returned to the Partington farm.

Mary persuaded her sisters to pool $360 for a Model T Ford with side curtains. Papa, at first, would have nothing to do with it. But Mary would later write in her family history: "Progress entered the Partington family with the Ford car."

Fig. 6. "Mary Partington, college graduation portrait" was the notation for this photograph in the 1908 Townsend Studio log book. Photograph by Timothy Townsend, courtesy of Townsend Studio, Lincoln, NE.

Fig. 7. Partington family portrait taken in 1923 after the death of Mary's mother, Ella Rhatigan Partington. Back row from left to right: Harold Partington, Anna Partington, Joseph Charles Richard Partington, Mary Ann Partington, James Harold Partington. Front row from left to right: Ella Grace Louise Partington, Mabel Margaret Partington, Hazel Alice Partington, Ada Elizabeth Partington. Photograph from the collection of Mary Ann Davis. Photograph by Dale, Lincoln, NE.

5.
How Shall We Say Goodbye

At about 9:30 on the night of April 13, 1923, Mabel and Grace started home from St. Patrick's in Havelock in the Model T. Temperatures in the forties had turned the snowy ruts into slush during the day but dropped again to the twenties. On the way home the Ford lurched to a stop in a muddy stretch.

Mary and her mother, Ella, walked down the road to meet the girls. Mary got in the car to steer while her mother helped push with the others.

Suddenly Mrs. Partington said she wasn't feeling right. "Overcome," she said. The girls helped her into the closest neighbor's, a Mr. Turks, so that she might rest. But Ella lived only a few minutes.

The newspapers of Havelock and University Place registered the shock of the community.

"A most exemplary mother," said The *University Place News*. "She was never known to speak ill of anyone." Gone was the stalwart supporter of education and many-termed president of the St. Patrick's Altar Society. "Highly esteemed in social and religious circles," said *The Havelock Post* of March 29th.

Harold Partington, now a widower with a large farm to manage, still had Joe, Mabel and Grace at home--Joe and Mabel in their late teens going to the University and Grace a high school senior at St. Patrick's. By this spring of 1923, James, the oldest son, had married Agnes O'Halloran. Ada, Hazel and Anna were married and teaching school in other cities. But Mary had given up teaching out of concern for her ailing mother.

Education was a strong value in the Partington children. Their mother, Ella, had attended Mount St. Joseph's Academy (renamed Clarke College in 1928) in Dubuque, Iowa, founded by an Irish immigrant. Mary Francis Clarke, the first Mother Superior, was by some indications a niece of Mary's maternal grandmother. The Academy was famous for its academic excellence with a strong bent toward the classics. All the Partington children except Grace had also attended University High with its emphasis on classics.

The children must continue . . .

Now, Mary, who had come home to help, had allowed her mother to push the car while she sat inside and steered. Mary sobbed out loud during the sermon.

The rest of the family sat in St. Patrick's and listened to Father D. O'Connor eulogize their mother and wife: "How shall we say goodbye? 'Tis hard to say farewell to thee as the last blasts of winter are departing, when the glory of spring is about to burst upon us with the beauty and fragrance of its flowers and the song and color of its birds. May this transition from winter's bleakness to spring's new life be but a symbol of the passing from temporal to eternal life."

"Mary screamed during the sermon," Neola Studnicka recalled. "She was hysterical and several men helped her out. The whole event was so sad. Everyone in the church started crying when Mary lost her composure. Mary and her mother were very close."

In 1923 a thirty-four year old unmarried daughter who was a school teacher was considered an old maid, a person without a real life of her own. She would now be expected to stay home and "take care of things."

Mary completed one semester of graduate work at the University of Nebraska in the summer of 1926.

While Mary did not abandon teaching--she continued to sub at St. Patrick's and elsewhere--she did not renew her teaching certificates or maintain her membership in professional organizations. She stayed on the farm to help her father with the family and home.

Great nephew Lee said, "Mary had a strong mothering instinct and felt she had to continue for her mother. I don't remember my grandmother (Ella), but all my dad's (James') brothers and sisters remained a close family throughout their lives. Mary had a definite role in maintaining this closeness through her life-long correspondence with her family and celebrating homecomings at the annual reunions."

"When bedtime came," said Mary Ann, "Aunt Mary would heat up rocks on the stove, wrap them in newspapers and carry them up to one of the beds and warm up the big feather tick. I'd get into bed and pretty soon she would come too and the bed would creak. She'd tell me stories until I fell asleep.

"When I grew older I'd walk out to Aunt Mary's. In springtime I'd pick all the strawberries I could eat. By the time I'd get back to the house, Mary would have gingerbread baked. We'd sit and have gingerbread and more strawberries and talk and laugh.

"We had a special relationship all my life. She was a dynamic woman with the most wonderful philosophy of life. One of the happiest people, yet she had so little. She just got more out of her simple life than any money could buy."

6. Dear Children, I Wish to Welcome You

Once Mary decided to stay on the farm on the outskirts of Lincoln, she hardly drove the car again, nor did she teach full terms. She pedaled her blue bike into Havelock when asked to substitute teach at St. Patrick's. When St. Patrick's closed in the late Twenties and reopened in the Thirties, Mary subbed again.

Former student Gerry Perkinton remembered:

"We loved it when Mary came to be our substitute. She spoke so clearly and always began the day with, 'Dear children, I wish to welcome you today.' Then she read us a story.

"The nuns at St. Patrick's also called on Mary to help with the annual Christmas pageant. Mary had a way of directing which seemed to bring the pageant together. She got us kids to do things well because she could make us feel good about ourselves. How proud we felt when she played the piano and we sang the Christmas carols."

"Aunt Mary," said namesake Mary Ann Kellogg, "believed anyone could do anything, because she had done things. She was a proud, resourceful woman--emancipated before her time. Perhaps one of the reasons Aunt Mary did not marry can be attributed to her boldness, her strong convictions and her lack of fear in stating her opinions which she had on a variety of subjects and issues.

"If a man were looking for a submissive woman he would not have found her in Aunt Mary."

"Mary Partington was my 4-H teacher," said Ann McManaman, "from 1927 to 1929. We were just a bunch of farm kids, but Mary respected us and made us believe we were the best. I won a first prize for my sewing project.

"Mary and I stayed good friends. Years later when my husband owned Jim's Airport Cafe at the crossroads of Highway 77 and Havelock Avenue, Mary often stopped in for a drink of water on her long bicycle ride to the farm."

Her photos show her as a big woman, dressed in dark clothes, making her bicycle look small. "It was an incongruous sight," Gerry Perkinton recalls, "and in a day when middle-aged women didn't ride bicycles.

"Mary came to Havelock to the gazebo in the park every time the Burlington Band held a concert. We noticed our friend, Mary, always alone, standing near a tree dressed in long skirts, high topped shoes, and hat propped on top of her wound up braids, listening with obvious enjoyment."

"She was a spinster," said Mary's friend, Nell McKinney. "Maybe Mary was afraid of men, but she never bothered to fix herself up. She did have beautiful eyes and a great laugh. Mary was terribly likable."

Mary's social connections were through volunteer work, Havelock Extension Club, 4-H, St. Patrick's and family gatherings.

"We went to Mary's sometimes," said Nell, "for our Extension Club lessons. These were lessons on homemaking such as canning, proper butchering and storage of chickens, and conservation of water used in the kitchen. Mary always had a nice lunch. She raised strawberries and we had strawberry preserves and breads."

"We hired Mary," recalled Elizabeth Fagan, "to stay nights with my aging parents. Mary walked or rode her bicycle from the farm to my parents' in Havelock. When weather was bad, my husband went to get her. She came about six p.m. and left in the morning after my parents got up and she had fixed them breakfast. Mary was a great woman and so proud of her heritage."

Mary at eighty-six, writing her family history, spoke of her parents. "We always paid cash and we owned the farm which our parents earned and paid for without inheritance. They raised eight children, educated them, and, they left the farm, tax free to their offspring.

"In the Abbott house, we ate our suppers by kerosene lights. No telephone, no radio, but we were as happy as we are now. Mama and Papa worked so hard to buy the land with their precious earnings so carefully saved."

"Aunt Mary," said Mary Ann, "frequently won first prize at the State Fair for her corn and sometimes for her jellies and jams."

In later years when she took up painting, she painted scenes from the farm and submitted those. A painting in grays and blues shows three sailboats moving through choppy water. Relatives and friends had frequently boated on the Partington Pond.

Mary's great nephew, James, recalls riding his bike out 27th street to the farm. "Aunt Mary's was a great place to visit for a ten-year old boy and his friends back then. We swam and fished in the lake back of the house. Sometimes we helped her weed the garden--potatoes and strawberries.

"In the evenings we would sit up listening to her tell us stories about 'the olden days' or we sometimes just talked. Mary was a great storyteller."

However, Mary also provided stories for her neighbors and strangers who saw her. Pedaling down the dirt road lined with sunflowers on hot, dusty afternoons, or crisp autumn days, Mary attracted attention.

A neighbor who lived on Mary's route said, "You couldn't help but notice her. Here she'd come, on that old bike, with those black tennis shoes, holding up an umbrella when it rained or when it got too hot. Mary dragged the past with her wherever she went."

Then Mary bought a herd of goats. The goats munched their way across the knoll at 44th and Superior, visible . . . and amusing to those who saw this as her latest eccentricity.

"Sure, Mary had a herd of goats," said her friend, Orville Smith. "Eight, maybe ten goats. Some thought the goats were a strange idea, but Mary knew what she was doing. The goats supplied her with milk, butter and cheese. If you know anything about bleu cheese you know the best comes from goat milk. She was compelled to live an economically simple life. She raised most of what she ate--chickens, vegetable garden, even made her own soap."

"When I was in high school," niece Mary Ann said, "it was the fashion to have mittens with fur on the back. I wanted a pair so badly. Aunt Mary butchered a goat and cured the hide. From this hide, she made me a pair of mittens with fur on the back for Christmas. Oh, how I loved and prized my Christmas gift."

When Mary Partington had guests, she took them into the parlor which was still kept just as her mother, Ella, had left it when she died in 1923. The dining room, with oak plate railings on each wall had china plates displayed, as also in the built-in oak china cabinet. Red carpet enriched the parlors, or living room and parlor.

The one she called the front room had the piano, a sofa chair of brown mohair and a curio cabinet. In the other stood leather furniture including the chaise lounge remembered as a favorite among nieces and nephews.

The kitchen at the northwest corner had a sink with a hand pump as well as a cook stove in which Mary burned corn cobs, wood and coal. Dark oak wainscoting mounted the kitchen walls.

Next to the kitchen was a small bedroom, across the hall a pantry.

Coming into Mary's house by way of the front door, a guest would notice the leaded glass window at the top of the landing--"an eye-catching sight," said nephew Lee. Another set of stairs led up from the kitchen hallway. Upstairs were five bedrooms, a bathroom and her father's recreation room with the pool table.

Below the kitchen a root cellar with a pull-up door on the north side sometimes doubled as a storm cave.

Mary enjoyed visitors and usually talked about her family's educational record, praising her brothers and sisters for achieving degrees--all but James who chose a business career. "He chose his own sort of education," Mary would say.

"Mary decided she was the mother of the family," said James' grandson Jack. "Her pioneer belief was that when you acquired land it was your duty to keep it in the family. Mary hosted the family reunions. One reunion when Mary had cooked for at least fifty people, I couldn't eat much. The well water made food taste odd and there was goat's milk in everything. But we had a great time together."

At these annual affairs, Mary would entertain with her family stories. "Remember when Anna fell out of the cherry tree and broke both her wrists? We had to take turns feeding her. Remember when Ada nearly died with the flu and lost her hair? How about the time Joe came downstairs in the dark and stepped in the crock of plum jam left there to cool? And poor Mama's teeth! They fell into the fire when she spit in the stove. Papa shot the tomcat after he bit the heads off those pure Maltese kittens. Remember Joe getting the rooster to fight himself in front of a looking glass?"

Mary gave of what she had worked for on the farm in those reunions, and at other times.

"One time I came home after several years for a visit," said great nephew James. "We went to the farm to see Aunt Mary. She was excited to see us and when it was time to leave, she gave the girls two Mason jars filled with coins. The girls kept their collections for years. That's how Mary was."

The priests at St. Patrick's knew that too, but Mary would come to them carrying fresh produce and cheese carried in bags attached to the handlebars of her bike.

Fig. 8. Untitled oil painting of boats painted by Mary Ann Partington in the 1930's. Painting from the collection of Mary Catherine Elsener.

Fig. 9. Untitled oil painting of shoreline painted by Mary Ann Partington in the 1930's. Painting from the collection of Mary Catherine Elsener.

7.
Percy Was Great

By 1935, only Harold Partington and his daughters, Mary and Mabel, lived in the farmhouse together. Joe, a Navy Commander, married and lived in Washington state. Grace, married to John Kellogg, Sr., lived in Lincoln.

Harold's will, written that year, appointed his oldest son James as executor and bequeathed his entire estate to be divided equally among his children.

All his life Harold maintained a strong loyalty to his homeland, England. At the time of George VI's coronation in December 1936, Harold hosted a gala celebration. For a week before, he flew the English flag from his front porch. The Partington family held a reception with Harold as host at Lincoln's Hotel Cornhusker. Harold talked of England that night, in his impeccable British accent.

Mary, however, did not attend.

When Harold's health began to fail, he rented out land north of the house. Some of his land reached all the way north to Arrow Airport. He hired his premium virgin hay mowed and marketed.

Two brothers with a garbage pickup service rented land down in the trees north of the Partington house. They bought pigs to eat garbage and their hired hand who tended pigs during the day came to be known as "Pigman" by the kids who went down the tree-shaded road to Salt Creek. The area with a darkly shaded dead-end road had an aura of mystery about it.

In the late Thirties, Harold developed diabetes and lost his sight. He often lay on the chaise lounge or in the bedroom off the kitchen. The syphon water system designed in 1907 stopped working. When Rural Electrification came through, the Partingtons chose to do without.

As his condition worsened, Harold moved into Lincoln to live with his son James. He died July 6, 1944 at seventy-nine, a member of University Episcopal Church. But Catholic Father O'Connor, who had conducted Ella's funeral, came from Bellwood to visit Harold's funeral and the family.

After Harold's death, Mary lived alone at the farm. Mabel had married and moved to Lincoln.

Before he died, Harold had deeded Mary tracts of land so she had a secure place to live.

During the 1940's she bartered the outbuildings on the farm for work--especially hay cutting. For years this exchange continued with the Aksarben race track remaining one of Mary's best customers of her prime prairie hay.

Mary tended her goats, chickens and garden. A nearby farmer rented land, used her buildings for cattle and did her heavy work.

During the war years Mary painted . . . and expressed her opinions. One scene depicted an air disaster of World War II. The painting brought her an award and local publicity. She submitted paintings to the State Fair.

Mary wrote public officials protesting the high duties on packages from her Aunt Lydia in England.

Mary made a public statement about Russia's reluctance to enter the United Nations after the War was over. She marched in a parade with a gold edged blue shawl and foot-high letters: U N and led her billy goat "Percy" wearing a drab belly-length denim with RUSSIA printed on both sides.

"Percy was great!" Mary said. "We won first prize, ten big dollars."

In the late 1950's the City of Lincoln began to annex the area north of Cornhusker Highway and south of the Partington farmstead. Mary's surroundings changed from farm community to suburban development. Nearby came ranch style houses decorated in black, aqua and pink. Television antennas brought the world into other's living rooms, but Mary chose not to go along. She liked Cornhusker and high school football on the transistor radio her brother James brought her, but that was as far as she went.

When the Salt Creek Diversion Project plans affected her Partington Pond, Mary urged members of her family to go with her to the June 4th, 1959, Sanitary Board. A clipping from the time says: "The Board sounded the death knell for an old landmark north of Lincoln (the Partington Pond). Mrs. Hazel Berigan, Miss Mary Partington and Harold Partington appeared for a hearing on a lake near 41st and Havelock Avenue called 'Partington Lake' which belongs to members of the Partington family . . . The lake will probably have to be drained and would dry up anyway even if the drainage project skirted around the lake."

The bed of this lake remains today, sloping northwest toward the woods, adjacent to Salt Creek.

8.
This Is Her World

Mary's big rawboned farmhouse stood alone on the hill like a windswept monument of another era. Somehow, the house looked unoccupied from the road where traffic hurried by. Those who stopped to visit her on a spring day would see the tulips blooming by the well.

In the Fifties baby boom neighbors reached out to Mary for child care. Mrs. Lillian Schmeiding said, "We chose Mary to babysit because there were few baby-sitters available and we knew she loved children. All of us were living out here in the country. In fact, until the Sixties all of this land north of Cornhusker was country. The City annexed some of the land, so many of us had to leave farming to choose different careers, because you can't farm city-taxed land.

"Mary didn't get caught in this deal because the land the Partington's owned wasn't included . . . when annexation occurred.

"Our children loved Mary," said Mrs. Schmieding, "because she played with them. She would get right down on the floor and play farm and auction with our son. And Mary also liked stories so she read to the children. Mary gave our daughter a copy of *Aesop's Fables* which she still cherishes. Mary also played the piano. We didn't have a piano so our daughter often went to Mary's to visit just to have a private concert.

"Mary wasn't one to have . . . coffee gatherings, but . . . one time when Mary's strawberry patch was full and ripe, she invited five of us neighbor ladies to a party. We had this lovely shortcake topped with a big mound of whipped cream. Then someone talked about the goats . . . This is silly, but I lost my appetite and couldn't finish the lovely dessert. I have always felt that I hurt my friend's feelings."

Another neighbor, Donna Barnell, recalled, "On summer afternoons when our girls were ten or eleven, they'd walk up to Mary's at least once a week for tea parties. They'd wait for me to finish a batch of cookies and when the cookies were ready, they'd pack a basket. Like Red Riding Hoods, they walked up the dusty road to Mary's for their visit. It was about a mile.

"When they returned home they were eager to share their story about the tea party. 'You know, she had to heat the water for tea on the old cook stove which is all she ever had in the kitchen. She made the tea herself!'

"The girls then set the table with (Mary's) mother's china. Mary and the girls would sit and visit for about an hour. Mary did love children and would entertain them as long as they wanted to stay."

Mary's delight with company and her ability to turn an ordinary event into a challenge delighted her niece, Mary Ann, who said:

"One time when I took my own children to see Aunt Mary, she told them, 'I don't have a car and cannot get into town to buy groceries . . . but I want you to come out and have dinner.

"I'm going to give you this money and I'd like you to shop for the dinner . . . You keep the change."

"Aunt Mary didn't want the event to be ordinary. We had hot dogs and smores and the children had a little bit of money left."

"When my daughter was getting married," said Nell McKinney, "we were entertaining when all of a sudden, there was Mary coming down the road on her bicycle, an umbrella stuck under her arm. She stopped, propped her bike up against a tree and clumped up the steps right into the living room wearing those big old tennis shoes she always wore. 'Here,' she said, 'I have this gift for your daughter.'

"Another time I came home and there, under the tree on a bench in our backyard, was Mary, sitting, eating a quart of ice cream. When I came out to talk to her she laughed and said,

'Hi. It's so darn hot, I just knew what a great spot this is to cool off and I knew you wouldn't mind.'"

"Mary," said another friend, "never forgot you for Christmas, St. Patrick's Day and Valentine's day. Her card might have the name erased from a former sender, but she never forgot you."

"Mary was a big woman," said Shannon Anderson, "with a kindly face and a cheerful way. I noticed her weathered look, the look of a person who has spent a lot of time outside. Her cheeks were round and pink when I met Mary in her yard. We were looking for her goats. I asked her why she didn't keep them penned up.

"She looked at me through her little round glasses and laughed. 'Oh,' she said, 'no need to pen them up. I never did hear of two goats who could decide to go in the same direction at the same time.'

"I remember looking around Mary's place. There was a homey, secluded look. Flowers bloomed around the windmill.

"I thought, this is her world. She can wake up in the morning and listen to the meadowlarks. She can walk down to the woods and see deer and families of pheasants.

"When I left Mary and drove back down toward Superior Avenue, I looked back and saw Mary standing in her yard with all those red hollyhocks by the windmill, three or four garments blowing on the clothesline and I thought, 'Now there's a strong individual.'"

9.
Like Rats in a Cheesecake

In the late Fifties, Mary Partington's home began having another kind of visitor. Young people drove their cars out, not to visit Mary, not on a friendly call, but to use the old dead end road that lead into the woods. Many who went by seeking adventure believed her old house abandoned.

Mary's place with no yard light, no electric lights inside, had little expression of life at night. The 44th Street dirt road lined with trees had a reputation as a parking spot because of its seclusion.

A few miles out in the country, away from the lights of the growing city, kids fresh from King's restaurant came to the crossroads of 44th and Superior and turned left toward the grove. Shrouded in huge oaks, ash and cottonwoods, the kids listened to the quiet of the country. Maybe the herd of goats in the yard knew the cars were there, but they kept still. Only the crickets refused to keep the silence. This was the perfect parking spot.

Perhaps on a dark night, someone in a car noticed a profile in an upstairs window of the old farmhouse. Mary had gotten up in the night. She heard something so she turned on her flashlight, casting a ghostly appearance. The kids in the car wondered if they had seen a ghost, or, worse, a real person.

Stories circulated about a woman called Bloody Mary. "She was said to be a total recluse," one man reported. "She was said to wear long white housecoats, giving her a ghostly appearance. One night I got to meet her at a safe distance. We were just passing by and saw a ghostly shape on the porch with something in her hands that looked like a shotgun. A hasty goodbye! That was the closest I ever came to the mystery lady."

"The whole thing," said Mary's neighbor Elton Rolofson, "started as an initiation rite for frat house residents from the University of Nebraska.

"Some of us neighbors, I recall, went up to Mary's one time to offer our help. She was very independent and never called on us, but some of us did call the sheriff's office several times when we heard a 'ruckus' up there."

Mary resolutely defended her rights to live in the home her parents had built and to be left alone.

On October 25, 1961, the Lancaster County Sheriff's Office received a call about 10 p.m.

from the Steak House at 33rd and Adams that someone had been shot at 44th and Superior and the "man was lying out in the yard."

Lt. Leitner and Sgt. Nowakowski immediately drove to Mary's yard and turned on the siren and dome light. They drove around the yard, searched the area including all the outbuildings and found nothing but goats in the yard. They searched the ditches north on 44th and then the ditches east and west on Superior Street. They dismissed the report as a hoax.

Someone had been shot at Mary Partington's address that night--Mary herself.

Earlier in the evening Mary, asleep in her upstairs room in the southwest corner of the house, awakened to the sound of glass breaking. She said, "I went to the window, opened it and yelled at the people outside. I raised the shade and a shot come through the window, hitting me in my stomach. I screamed, 'I'm shot. I'm shot!'

"I heard a car drive away and went downstairs to light a lamp. I could feel blood running down my leg. I took a cloth, wiped off the blood and then got another cloth, put liniment on it and put it over the wound. I went back upstairs. It didn't hurt too bad. Later I heard the patrol car in the yard, but I was too tired to get up again."

The next morning a woman from a trailer park on Cornhusker Highway came looking for her runaway dog. Mary told the woman about the shooting. This unidentified woman left

Mary's, made phone calls and Mary was later taken to St. Elizabeth's Hospital.

A Lincoln physician confirmed that he had removed "what was apparently a .22 caliber rifle slug from Miss Partington's stomach on October 26th, 1961, at St. Elizabeth's Hospital." Mary told the sheriff that she had been shot after kids had stoned her house. "They drove off when they heard me scream."

Two weeks later, November 9, 1961, Mary wrote to the Public Mind of the *Lincoln Journal* an article published under the title "Harassment."

"I have not complained to the police for 'ten or twelve years' as the sheriff's office reported (Lincoln Journal, 11/7/61), but I have been harassed for only about twenty-five months.

"True, I did not report the shooting at about 10 p.m. on October 25, but someone did because the police car came, circled my house and drove off without stopping. Sheriff Karnopp said on October 27 that the officers did not hear me yell to them from raised windows on the north, west and south.

"The woman who took me to Lincoln was a complete stranger.

"And I do have window curtains and blinds.

"It is too bad to have all this hullabaloo over persistent 'funsters' bent on teasing an old woman. I have tried to reason, appeal, shame and persuade my unknown antagonists, but like rats in a cheesecake, they come back.

"Who can straighten this out?

"I am out real money: doctor, hospital, three house window panes, plus two storm windows, roof trouble, etc. . .

"Maybe the gunman thought the house was empty, but I was abed at 10 p.m. when he began to throw stones and shoot.

"I challenge that excuse. These tormenters know better than that for they call me by name. What would you do?"

After this incident in 1961, Mary's brother James and her sister Grace and her family convinced Mary that a phone was a necessity for her to summon help. A phone with an unlisted number was installed downstairs on the wall near the kitchen.

About this time, Mary acquired a gun. Several accounts tell about the acquisition of the shotgun. Mary began to use it to scare intruders away. One story has it that a group of neighbors visited Mary with the gun and gave her lessons.

One family member thinks the gun may have been around the farm in one of the out-buildings because rattlesnakes were once prevalent.

"My uncles and great uncles," Jack Partington remembers, "used to shoot rattlesnakes out at the farm and nail the rattles up on the wall. The gun was probably around and Mary put it back into use."

Mary wrote about using a gun many years before when she saw her youngest sister staring, fascinated, at a rattlesnake coiled near the porch.

"I ran for the shotgun," Mary said in her family history, "and aimed. In a moment's blast, the snake was in pieces and Grace continued to ride her tricycle around the cement walk."

Mary told members of the sheriff's department she needed the gun "in case I want to go out into the woods to shoot a rabbit for my dinner."

Paul Douglas, County Attorney, said that Mary was not in abuse of the law owning a shotgun because she made no attempt to conceal it.

Sgt. Monroe of the Lancaster County Sheriff's Office reminisced about going to Mary's to check reports of vandalism:

"I remember going to Mary's often. I always went to the front door of her home to visit with her. She was a big, heavyset woman with a kind expression. Who believed she had a right to be left alone.

"Some officers viewed Mary as a crank, a bothersome person making up a lot of stories because it was after things happened out there that we would arrive. Some officers preferred not to go to Mary's place because she had the shotgun and aimed at cars trespassing on her property.

"We made a deal with her. We agreed that when we came into her yard, we would turn on the red dome light. That way she would know it was help and not vandals.

"I was pretty sure Mary was telling the truth about being harassed because there were gunshot holes all over the outside of her house. There were also broken windows."

In November, 1961, after Mary had been shot, one of her neighbors, Mrs. Betty Sundberg, wrote to the Public Mind in defense of her neighbor:

"Recently I stopped to talk with Mary Partington. She had walked to the corner to put her mailbox on its post to mail a letter to the sheriff.

"It is a federal offense to tamper with the United States mail boxes, yet Miss Partington tells me that to keep from having it destroyed, she has to take it in each day after the mail goes.

"What would you readers do if repeatedly your home was fired at with guns and someone called you names and told you they wanted your home? Miss Partington tells me she has spent more than $100 replacing windows in the past year."

In her family history, Mary wrote about the young people swarming to the farm which she called Valhalla, for fun in the early 1900's. In the 1960's, young people again swarmed to Valhalla with a different definition of fun: teasing an old woman alone in an old farmstead.

Fig. 10. View of the east side of the Partington house. Taken the day after the Earl Eldon Hill shooting by the *Lincoln Evening Journal* (October 26, 1966, page 1). Reprinted, by permission, from Lincoln Journal-Star, Lincoln, NE.

Fig. 11. Partington family photograph taken in 1957. From left to right: Hazel Alice Partington Berigan, Joseph Charles Richard Partington, Mary Ann Partington, James Harold Partington, Ada Elizabeth Partington Greusel, Ella Grace Louise Partington Kellogg, Mabel Margaret Partington Knox. Photograph from the collection of Lee and Carol Partington. Photographer unknown.

10.
Common Decencies Are Becoming Frail

Between October 25, 1961, and late October, 1966, the Lancaster County Sheriff's office responded to calls at Mary Partington's regarding shots to her windows, rock throwing, fires set on her porch, and a tree cut down and placed in front of her home, her outhouse overturned, burglarizing, an unknown male blindfolding and tying her up, holding a gun to her head, and demanding food, then stealing items and money from her. One night she awakened to find a young woman standing at the foot of the bed.

Mary's nephew, Jack Partington, remembers:

"This bum came in the house and tied Mary up. He demanded she tell him where he could find food in the cupboards, which she did. She talked with him until he finally left. She was probably too much for him, although he claimed he was an escapee from Alcatraz."

During these years of trouble for Mary, she also had her mind on other things. In July 1963 she wrote the Public Mind about the new music coming over her transistor:

"Where in the world is our music going? The men and the women on the air pour out tones and words that would startle Santa Claus.

"The orchestras specialize in bean bags, whistles, thumps, pig grunts and sound like the picture window being struck by lightning.

"If 'America' or 'Annie Laurie' or any honest to goodness tunes are chosen, they are all bopped up. No wonder our generations are impatient, non-religious, going 'all the way' somewhere without a thought of where to."

In September, 1964, Mary wrote another letter to the Public Mind about discrimination.

"Discrimination is mankind's burden," Mary wrote.

"What fat girl is besieged with dates? The only garment tailors turn out perfectly for fat men is a night shirt.

"The father of ten children looking for a house to rent cannot depend on his constitutional rights to his 'pursuit of happiness' entirely."

Mary may have had a particular family in mind when she wrote about the father with ten children. She was also losing patience by this time with those who threatened her own constitutional rights--rights to the safety and peace of her home. She picked up her gun more often, opening her upstairs windows to warn intruders in her yard that they were trespassing. When the trespassers refused to leave and she fired her gun, that seemed to be the reaction some of the kids wanted.

On September 18, 1964, Mary heard a noise about 11:30 p.m. She got up, looked out her upstairs bedroom window and saw several cars parked next to her kitchen porch. She ordered the trespassers to leave. They hollered back and threw rocks at her window. She fired her shotgun through the window. A teenage girl sitting in the back seat of one of the cars was hit in the shoulder, neck and chest.

After an investigation of the shooting, the intruders, including the injured girl, admitted they had parked their cars on the north side of the house, had gotten out and were raising a rumpus. "When we thought we saw someone at the window," one said, "we got scared and ran to our cars. Then the shot hit the window, shattered it and, sure enough, someone got hurt."

No charges were filed against Mary because the parties were trespassing and had vandalized her home.

A few days after the incident, Mary wrote again to the Public Mind: "It is a burning shame that trespassing and destructive citizens in this city of colleges make it necessary to put up 'Keep Off' signs on my suburban property. Common decencies are becoming frail."

Twenty years later, certain people who went out to Mary's between 1961 and 1966 described their experiences and feelings about what they did and why they went. With two decades of retrospection, they had insight into a time once seen as fun, into a thrill they couldn't find anywhere else.

"I went out to Mary's," one said. "I was an undergrad at the University and a bunch of us had heard so many tales about Mary and the Pigman that we decided to go out. Some of us sat on the hood of the car chanting, 'Bloody Mary, Bloody Mary, Pigman, Pigman! Come on out!'

"All of a sudden! Whoosh! Out of a tree hanging over the car came this creature right on to the shoulders of one of the guys I was with. I really don't remember how we got out of there. That was the one and only time I ever went out to Mary's. We all believed the guy who jumped out on us was the Pigman."

Jack Partington, Mary's nephew said, "Whenever I heard any story about kids going out to Mary's, my friends and I made a point of driving by more often. On one of these occasions, a buddy and I went out there dressed in fatigues, carrying M-1's. We were on our way to practice at the rifle range, so, as we drove north on 44th Street, we noticed a couple of cars parked in Mary's yard with some kids yelling. We sneaked up on those kids with those M-1's posed. You can't believe how those kids shook and got out of there fast!"

Mary Elsener when she was about ten recalled going out to her Great Aunt Mary's with her father and Grandpa James Harold Partington:

"Mary took me and my brother into the dining room and showed us the bullet holes in her walls. You can imagine how wide eyed we were when she said to us, 'Look! Just look at this! This is what some kids do out here!'

Another person who went to Mary's to "raise thunder" said:

"Five or six of us went out to Bloody Mary's. I was the brave one. I stayed in the car. There was a chain across the yard. The idea was to go through the chain and up on her porch to sneak a look in the window.

"While my friends sneaked through the fence and went toward the house, I sat in the car that quiet, dark night, waiting. Soon I heard the sound of a window opening and a voice shouting, 'Stop or I will shoot.'

"My friends, being at that silly age, hollered, 'Say please, say please.'

"Gunshots filled the night. You never saw so many kids get in a car and take off in a hurry. That was the only time I went out there."

An antique collector remembers visiting a bachelor friend and seeing an elegant creamer and sugar bowl on his table. "The set seemed so out of place, I inquired," he said. "You will never believe this, but years ago I sneaked into Bloody Mary's house and I stole it. That was the dare in those days, to go in and steal things and get out before she heard you and started shooting. Lots of my friends have trophies . . . "

Another Lincoln resident told this story:

"If you were a kid in the Sixties and lived in Northeast Lincoln, you went out to Bloody Mary's. It was eerie because the house was always dark. We stole a carburetor once from Pigman."

Another said, "Going out to Bloody Mary's was what you did back then to find a thrill. We kept going until we discovered sex."

Mary Partington's note to the sheriff's department June 19, 1962, said: "On Friday, (June 15) about 4 p.m., a car went past this house and down beyond the barn and I mistook it for the man who waters the cattle. He did not stop here or return so I went to look.

"Down on the ground, beneath the cottonwood, a shapely female, bare 100%, leg weaved. It was car (license plate number). As the man buttoned up, his glare at me was full, defiant and steady.

"Today I found a beer bottle , only one, and Kleenex used to wipe off blood. The young woman held her hand to her face as they left. I would guess him at anywhere around 30 years old and not hungry. I am not much of a judge of ages, but her leg was spring chicken type and no old hen's.

"So now it's daytime too! * !"

The note was signed, "Mary Partington."

While Mary continued to suffer harassment, she never gave up on youth. In a response to an editorial of May 31st, 1965, Mary wrote to the Public Mind: "I agree with your May 31st editorial, 'Jobs for the Young' that our fine young people should be given jobs. They need money even if they are only bound for recreation. I'm sure everybody would like to see these future lawmakers gainfully employed. Personally I am short of money and push-button machinery which seems to hamper me in the do-gooder field."

On July 27, 1965, Mary again wrote the Lincoln Journal: "Religion embodies forth worship, love and obedience to God regardless of creed . . . when it comes to God's laws given to Moses, it causes squirming even in the Church. For humanity, many never think of God, much less worship Him. Keeping God's day holy is uncommon. Parental 'honor' ends up in a nursing home manned by strangers. Humanity often murders, cheats and lies . . . covets both neighbors' goods and wives (and husbands) . . . Are we slipping, or just gone soggy?"

Mary's brother James visited her often, taking food and fuel to her. Sometimes he took her to family affairs.

John Kellogg, Jr., said of this period, "Aunt Mary often spent Sundays with my family in Lincoln. We picked her up in the morning and in the evening we took her home where she would light her oil burning lamps. We made sure she was okay.

"She never seemed afraid to go to the farm, even though it was a big house and would have scared most people to live there alone. I guess she just learned to live alone and be self-sufficient because she never married, but she certainly was not anti-social as she was active in her church and corresponded with her many brothers and sisters. Generally Mary loved people.

"Mary liked living alone even when she was in apparent danger, because she loved the farm and was used to her life there. Because of her faith, she did not fear people and basically trusted God's provident care and protection."

But, by October 1, 1966, Mary Partington was obviously fed up. She pleaded to be left alone in this note to the Lincoln Journal:

"What do you young people want? The night prowling with intent to maim and destroy is childish. This land should be ashamed of the guerilla assaults on people who have never done harm to you.

"Air your grievances to the elected or appointed officials invested to act. Aren't you willing to live and let live?"

This letter above appeared only twenty-five days before the article, "Intruder Is Slain by Elderly Woman," appeared in the October 26th edition of the *Lincoln Star*.

The prolonged series of troubles at the farm worried Mary's brother James. But James lay in the hospital the tragic night when Mary killed Earl Eldon Hill, October 25th.

Mary was grief-stricken at her brother's funeral in December. James had been one of her best friends. They had many things in common, especially their sense of humor. Lee recalled how they laughed, how his father kept everyone's spirits up with his rare humor.

Mary had a quiet winter of 1966-67. She seemed to spend little time dwelling on the sadness. Mary Ann Kellogg said, "Aunt Mary didn't talk much about the shooting incident. She had a way of accepting what happened in her life, including this incident. Definitely she experienced sorrow about it, but under the circumstances she had no other way to protect herself and her home."

Mary continued several more years living alone in what she had always considered "the most wonderful farmhouse in Lancaster County."

Fig. 12. Photograph of Mary Ann Partington taken at a family gathering in the 1970's. Photograph from the collection of John H. Kellogg, Jr. Photographer unknown.

11.
Natives of Havelock Were Sociable

During the late 1960's, one of Mary's projects was writing the history of St. Patrick's Parish in Havelock. Mary often went to Mass when the school children attended and then walked over to the rectory where she worked on her writing.

She traced the parish from its beginning as a mission church. In the 1890's, she said, a traveling priest celebrated Mass in farm homes including the Partington's.

Mary wrote: "Natives of Havelock, once called Salt Creek, were sociable people with not one but three dance halls."

She went on to tell how St. Patrick's frame church burned to the ground in 1907. Flaming excelsior had fallen from the open door of the pot bellied stove. The soft excelsior, scavenged from a crate, had been used to create a cot for the pastor to sleep in the sacristy. The St. Patrick's fire ignited seven other buildings in Havelock.

Mary went on to tell of the $28,000 church and school built in 1908, of the suffering among Burlington railroad families and farm families in the Depression, of the auctioning of St. Patrick's Church on the east steps of the Lancaster County Courthouse, and of how Bishop Kucera found an anonymous donor in Chicago who loaned $16,000 to the parish to restore the church to its congregation.

For her history, Mary researched and remembered the early Twentieth Century attitudes toward Irish immigrants. The Klu Klux Klan was strong in the area. "While the Catholics were holding an enjoyable dance," she wrote, "men came running up shouting that the KKK (Klu Klux Klan) were burning a cross in front of the dance hall. Jim Cudahay became a hero because he grabbed the burning cross and threw it across Havelock Avenue where it landed in front of a gas pump, (no explosion). Jim had a room on the third floor of the church to guard the property for a long while after that."

During those days of working on the history, Mary walked or rode her bicycle to Havelock. John and Bob Allington started ISCO Manufacturing east of Mary's. John said, "When either Bob or I saw Mary walking toward Havelock, one of us would jump in our car to offer her a ride. I'd say to myself, 'Oh, the poor old gal!' I couldn't bear it. She was always so appreciative of these rides.

"My wife and I picked her up two different times to take her to the ISCO picnics. She invited us into her parlor which looked like a room out of the historical society. To us Mary was a self-sufficient woman, full of confidence, but I suppose she appeared eccentric.

"About 1970, Bob and I finally convinced Mary to sell us her hay meadow. This was really three parcels of land which she had hung on to."

Mary's troubles were visible because of the broken windows, the yard littered with beer cans and the house defaced with red painted obscenities.

The Orville Smiths often picked up Mary on her way to church. "When we dropped her off after church at her farm," Orville said, "we would remind her to wait for us on the corner the next Sunday. Mary had an unlisted phone number so we couldn't call her, and we knew she would never call us to ask for a ride, so we made a point of keeping an eye out for her on Sundays."

Steve O'Hare, who was Mary's friend since he was a little boy, said that he discovered the woods behind Mary's was one of the best for hunting.

"Mary was happy to grant permission to hunters if they remembered to ask for permission. Mary didn't like acts of disrespect. I visited her home many times and, to show you how trusting she was, she never locked her door. Several times I just walked in and went through the house until I found her. She scolded me just like I scold my son now for an act of disrespect. Mary had a strong sense of right and wrong.

"Mary was intelligent," said Steve, "and a reader. She held progressive views about what was happening in the world. When I was in high school, I often went to Mary's to have her help me clarify some issue we had discussed in history or political science.

"After I got married, my wife and I often went to Mary's. When we told her we were going to have a baby, she was thrilled and we had a good time when Mary suggested names.

"Sometimes I went to Mary's to see if I could help her," Steve said. "I carried coal and cobs for her and helped her with her well. Once in a while, the well froze up in the winter. We worked together on those cold winter days until we got it going.

"One time, one of my best friends, one of the guys who sometimes went with me to hunt on Mary's land, went on a raid to Mary's. I knew he had gone. He knew that I knew he had gone, but we just could not ever talk about it.

"Mary was a survivor. Her relationship with her home was a commitment. Mary became a part of the land, a strong character in the story her parents had begun."

Some argued that when Mary chose to be different as she did, in her dress, in her solitude, in her independence, she attracted attention. The folly which led to the war between Mary and the thrill-seekers was a shared folly--dressed in dark, outdated clothing, raising goats, riding a bicycle, refusing electricity, Mary had made herself notorious as an anachronism. She was famous and people wanted to get close to the legend.

Curiously, during the very time of her harassment by one type of youth, she was a friend of others. One junior high student in the early Seventies said, "We used to drive out to Bloody Mary's in the dark, just to see what it was like and, yes, it was spooky. I (also) had a girl friend who took me to Mary Partington's to visit after school. To my surprise Mary was a nice old lady. We sat in her old-fashioned living room while she showed us pictures of her family in old albums. She also talked to us about her trouble with window peekers."

In a letter to family members in the early Seventies Mary wrote:

"Dear Ones All and Celia,

"My Fourth (of July) was so full and happy throughout from farm to return. It was a great day.

. . .

"Who mows your yard? No high wild oats there (in your yard) as in my rural setting. But I do have a fine red hollyhock in flower plus a big elderberry bush going into fruit.

"Now God bless us all and keep 'prosperity' among us.

. . .

"Aunt Mary"

12.
I Had to Pay for Independence

Mary worked for years on her own manuscript, a collection of historical documents and family stories as her effort to "preserve the Partington family heritage." She finished her booklet and gave it as Christmas gifts to family members in 1976. Part of what she wrote is interwoven here.

By 1975 Mary's health began to fail. Neighbors saw her using a cane on her walks to St. Patrick's--her sanctuary and her social connection.

"It was a hot summer day," said Nell McKinney, "when Mary fell over at the communion railing at St. Patrick's. I was right next to her when she fainted. I believe she was overcome. My husband helped her outside."

Other friends recall their last visits with Mary at her farm.

John Cejka, who lived nearby, said, "Our son had gone up to visit Mary. Back in the woods behind Mary's house a German shepherd had given birth to six white puppies. Our son ran home to beg my wife and me to come see. He ran ahead of us and I shall never forget the sight when I found Mary, our son and those little white pups. There they were, the old lady and the little kid, trying with all their might to keep the mosquitoes off the pups. My wife and I knew from the looks in their eyes that we had to take the pups home. Mary could not care for them."

Gerry Perkinton, who had loved Mary as a substitute teacher years before, recalled a terrible storm one summer night. "A nest of turtle doves we had been watching had fallen out of the tree in our yard. One of the doves had a broken wing. I was beside myself as to what we could do with the bird because we had cats. Then it came to me. Mary's!

"Now, I had not been out to Mary's since before the shooting. I asked my daughter to come along because, honestly, I was a little wary to go. Mary might think we were trespassing.

"My daughter and I put the birds in our car and drove over to Mary's. We honked and honked and pretty soon she came out the door. I waved from the car and yelled, 'Hi Mary. Do you remember me?'

"I remember thinking, 'She has not changed one bit. She looks just the same.' She was so happy to see us and I showed her the little bird.

"Mary looked at the bird and said, 'Oh, come with me. I know just the perfect place for the poor little broken thing.'

"Mary got her cane and we went out back to the trees. She gently put the bird in a tree. 'It will be just fine there,' she said. And the way she said it assured me.

"That's how Mary was. Maybe Mary was like the bird. The years must have wounded her. In spite of all her trouble, she had found her safe place and stayed right there."

Before the winter of 1976, Mary's youngest sister Grace fell ill. Grace and John had been a strong force in allowing Mary to remain on the farm. They came often to take her shopping, out to eat, to church and to their Lincoln home.

Grace's illness brought her daughter Mary Ann home to Lincoln. Mary Ann had a special relationship with Aunt Mary. She said, "When I saw that mother would not get well, I went out to the farm and said, 'Aunt Mary, you have to have help here. You know Mother won't be able to come out to help you. While I am here, I'd like to find a good place for you to live in Lincoln.'

"I think," said Mary Ann, "Aunt Mary recognized her vulnerability because she advised me she would consider a move. I spent a week and finally found a room in a big, old lovely home with the Ingersons at 3246 'S' Street. It would not be like home, of course, not like the farm, but comfortable.

"Mary moved into a large sunny room which had a large picture window for her to look out. It was an affordable solution for Aunt Mary.

"Mr. and Mrs. Ingerson were marvelous to her. Mr. Ingerson called her Miss Mary and he brought her meals and two snacks each day.

"It was at this time that I got Aunt Mary a recorder. She used it to communicate with me because reading and writing were becoming difficult for her. I also ordered tapes from the Nebraska Library Commission Books for the Visually Impaired. How she loved it! Aunt Mary, an avid radio fan all her life from her first crystal set to her transistor, easily converted to a recorder fan. She ordered tapes on politics, literature and poetry.

"Aunt Mary felt fortunate to have lived through the era she had, seeing transportation progress from horse and buggy to cars, trains and planes.

"She had her first plane ride after Mother died. She came with my dad from Lincoln to Denver. Although she boarded the planes in a wheelchair, she enjoyed the experience. The stewardesses gave her a pair of first flight wings which thrilled her."

While Mary lived with the Ingersons, she and her family agreed to put the farm at 44th and Superior up for sale. Before the farm sold, Mary moved to Madonna Nursing Home because she had fallen and broken her hip.

Mary's house was now truly an abandoned farmhouse. Although the family had moved the furniture out and Mary had given china and glassware to nieces and nephews, the vandals still came, sometimes in pickups. They stripped out the oak wainscoting, the oak in the staircase and other woodwork. They took fixtures.

The Partingtons hired Crawford Lumber Company of Lincoln to tear the house down.

On June 23, 1977, came the ultimate act of vandalism: arsonists set fire to the porch. Flames raced up into the second floor. The top floor fell into the bottom floor. Soon after the fire, the Partington family hired a crew of bulldozers to raze the area with orders to restore the little knoll to a plowed field state.

"The news of the fire affected Aunt Mary," Mary Ann Kellogg said, "but she simply refused to dwell on the tragic aspects of life. She lived as always with her attitude that life is for the living and we must go on."

"Mary Partington was a prayerful, holy lady," said Sister Enid Dodge, who worked at Madonna while Mary lived there. "She was pretty, too, with her reddish strawberry hair.

"She had a face of goodness and never complained about a thing. She had a few religious artifacts, but Mary didn't need much. She struck me as a person who always did what she could where she was with what she had.

"Mary had a good sense of humor too. I used to say to her, 'How could you be the lady the kids called Bloody Mary?'

"Mary would laugh and say, 'I guess that's the price I had to pay for independence.'"

"Aunt Mary maintained her trait of being interested in others," Mary Ann Kellogg said. "Even when things got a little hazy toward the end, she never chose an attitude of 'Oh, poor me, look at me.' She asked about you until the day she died."

In June, 1979, Mary's old friend and former student from high school days, Mrs. Elizabeth Fagan, stopped in at Madonna to visit a friend. While there she overheard someone say, "Mary Partington is tired and wants to go to bed."

"I looked around," Elizabeth said, "and there, in a wheelchair, was my old friend, Mary! A nurse nearby told me I could talk with her.

"During the conversation the ninety-year old Mary said to me, "Oh, Elizabeth, I so want to live to be a hundred."

"I asked, 'Why?'

"She answered, 'I want to see how many more changes will come.'"

Mary lived only a few more days. Early in the morning of June 14th, the woman who had fought for life and dignity so many years, announced, "I think I will die today."

Mary wheeled herself into her room, said the "Our Father" and died.

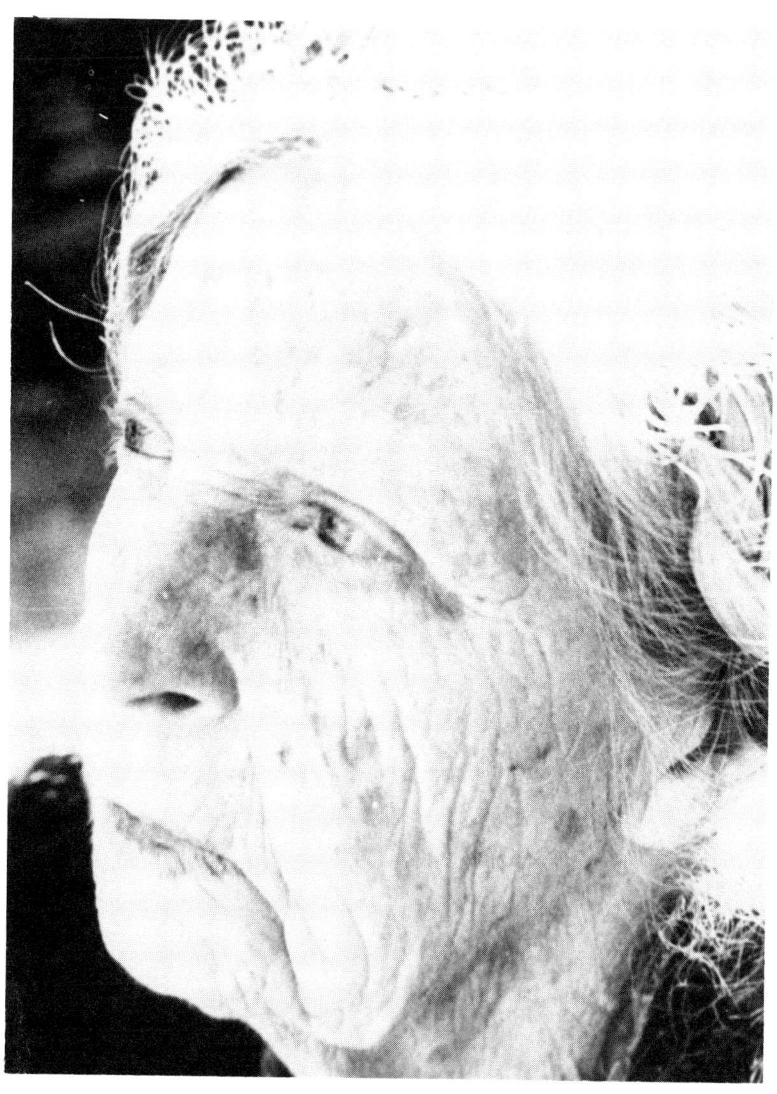

Fig. 13. Photograph of Mary Ann Partington was taken in Evergreen, CO, by Mary's great niece for a photography class assignment on aging in 1976. Photograph by Nancy Davis Richardson.

Fig 14. View of south side of Mary Ann Partington's house after the arsonist's fire destroyed the building (*The Lincoln Star*, August 11, 1977). Reprinted, by permission, from The Lincoln Journal-Star, Lincoln, NE.

13.
She Always Spoke Highly of It

Perhaps few readers of the *Lincoln Journal* on June 14, 1979, made the connection between the death notice of Mary Partington and the woman of the legend.

However, Mary's will caused a headline in the *Lincoln Star* on March 11, 1980. "Lincolnite's Bequest Surprises College."

The article stated: "Miss Partington, who died last June at the age of 90, was convinced that her grandmother had been related to Mother Mary Frances Clarke who founded the college in 1843.

"Miss Partington's sister, Mabel Knox of Lincoln, said her grandmother, Anne Clarke, was born in Dublin, Ireland, in 1826, and emigrated to the U. S. as a young girl.

"Her family settled in Bernard, a small town about fifteen miles southwest of Dubuque. Eventually she married a man named Rhatigan and had children, including their mother, Ella.

"Ella Rhatigan eventually moved to McCook, Neb., then to Lincoln, where she met and married a man named Partington. They had eight children, including Miss Partington and Mrs. Knox.

"Miss Partington was a school teacher for most of her life.

"Mrs. Knox said her sister had been told that their grandmother, Anne Clarke, was closely related to Mother Clarke, foundress of the college and its religious order, the Sisters of Charity, Blessed Virgin Mary.

"Miss Partington wrote to Clarke officials hoping to establish her grandmother's exact relationship to Mother Clarke. Although Mother Clarke also had emigrated from Ireland in the 1830s and had settled in Dubuque County, college officials were unable to establish a definite link.

"But that didn't stop Miss Partington from feeling something very special about Clarke College, Mrs. Knox said.

"'Mary had great affection for Clarke College,' she said. 'She always spoke so highly of it.'

"Miss Partington's will bequeathed small amounts to a relative and a church and left $20,200 each to Clarke and the Creighton University medical school."

Before Mary Partington died, she asked her niece, "Mary Ann, do you believe a person should leave their money to relatives?"

"Only," said Mary Ann, "if you owe someone something should you leave them money."

"Mary Ann," her aunt went on, "I would like to leave my money to Clarke College, even if I don't have very much."

Much of the money Mary bequeathed Clarke, Creighton and St. Patrick's may have come from the sale of her hay meadow to ISCO Manufacturing Company east of her old home.

The real Mary Partington, as opposed to the legend, was a woman who made her own history. Writing her story, collecting her family and church history, writing to newspapers, public officials, her family and friends, she made her impression.

Mary affirmed the Havelock church and community which held out open arms for Irish Catholic families, so Mary felt at home there. And she affirmed Catholic education.

Mary's grand niece, Mary Catherine Elsener, in a 1986 University of Nebraska course assignment to write about "someone unusual," wrote:

My Aunt Mary

Bloody Mary was famous
round these parts.
She wasn't bloody, only Mary.
A large woman
old fashioned to see
hair scalloped around her face
(hair) pulled tight in a ball
a sack-straight print dress
down way below her knees
and big cloppy shoes
a face not lined but
smooth for her years
once pretty perhaps
deep booming voice
sharp wit, quick mind
that sometimes spilled
poetry and pretty painted pictures.
Her once grand house
was tired and cracked
no longer held children,
laughter or love
only time and Mary.
A large house
old fashioned to see
no running water
nor electricity.
The house kept peeling
its dead skin
all those years
yet you could see
it was once pretty perhaps.

People called Mary crazy
and made up great lies
of ghosts and pigmen and
strange strange happenings.
The young teased and taunted
the old lady
they shot out the windows
she showed me the bullets
in her faded gray walls
and two in her belly.
She took care of herself.
She once shot a man
blew off his face
when he crawled through her
window in the dark country night.
So they called her Bloody Mary
stealing peace and privacy.
They made up fool stories
about a crazy old lady who wasn't.
After she left they burned
the old house to the ground
a house of my roots.

On the little knoll a minute's walk northwest of 44th and Superior, a visitor may find on a summer day a cement rectangle brimming with purple musk thistles, little blue stem and gramma grass. Many times I have visited the knoll where Mary lived. I have seen no ghost on any of these visits. I have, however, come to know the spirit of a person who lived her life in her own way and was willing to pay the price.

Epilogue

The Partington family sold the remaining land of their estate to the Lincoln Foundation. In 1983, the Lincoln Foundation along with an anonymous donor bequeathed this land to the City of Lincoln. Eventually this land will be part of Crescent Greens Park, part of the larger Helen Boosalis Park.

The area will one day bring young people back for recreation. The Partington Pond, of affectionate memory in the family, will be given new form and filled with water.

Fig. 15. Mary Ann Partington's gravestone. Photograph from the collection of the author.

Select Time Line

This time line of events in the life of Mary Ann Partington is incomplete. Many of the records have been destroyed, misplaced, or not released.

-- Stephen K. Hutchinson, compiler

1806, Mar. 2	Mary Frances Clarke born in Dublin, Ireland
1826	Ann Clarke Rhatigan (Ella's mother) immigrates to the United States from Dublin, Ireland
1833	Mary Frances Clarke and four Sisters of Charity arrive at St. Michael's school and convent in Philadelphia, PA, from Dublin, Ireland.
1843	St. Michael's burns, Mary Frances Clarke and sisters move to Dubuque, IA, and establish St. Mary's Academy (*forerunner of Clarke College*)
1865, Feb. 28	Harold Partington born, Lancashire, England
1865, Dec. 4	Ella Rhatigan (Partington) born, Bernard, Dubuque, Co., IA
1879	After a series of name changes St. Mary's Academy is renamed Mount St. Joseph's Academy.
1885, May 5	Harold Partington emigrates from Liverpool, England, to U. S. on the ship "Adriatic"
1887, Oct. 21	Harold Partington and Ella Rhatigan married, Lincoln,NE
1889, Mar. 22	Mary Ann Partington born
1891, Feb. 15	James Harold Partington born
1892, Dec. 19	Ada Elizabeth Partington (Greusel) born
1893, Jan.	St. Patrick's Parish organized
1893, July 30	30' x 60' building completed for St. Patrick's Church
1895, Dec. 8	Hazel Partington (Berigan) born
1897, Dec. 13	Anna E. Partington (Shannon) born
1900, Feb. 2	Joseph Charles Richard Partington born
1901	Harold Partington begins buying land
1902, June 12	Mabel Partington (Knox) born
1902-04	Mary attends University Place High, University Place, NE (*completed 10th grade*)
1904	Construction begins on Partington farmhouse
1904, Nov. 30	Ella Grace Louise Partington (Kellogg) born
1906	Construction completed on Partington farmhouse, family moves in
1907	Fire destroys St. Patrick's Church building

1908	Construction begins on new St. Patrick's Church building
1908-09	Mary attends University Place High, University Place, NE (*Mary filled out the registrar's card 9-20-15, she said she attended Nebraska Wesleyan University for 2 years, possibly to finish her junior and senior years in high school*)
1910-11	Mary teaches, District 134, Waverly, NE
1911, Oct. 28	Harold Partington fills out "Petition for Naturalization"
1912, Jan. 27	Harold Partington granted U.S. citizenship
1913,n.d.	James Harold Partington marries Agnes
1911-13	Mary teaches, District 86, Norwood Park, Havelock, NE
1915, "early"	Mary stays with relatives in St. Paul, MN
1915, Mar. 1	Mary teaches, Max,MN
1915, June	Mary finishes term in Max and leaves MN
1915-18	Mary attends University of Nebraska, Lincoln, NE
1916, Sep.	St. Patrick's Church school established
1918, May 27	Mary receives AB degree and University Teacher's Certificate, University of Nebraska
1918-19	Mary teaches, junior high, Lewiston, NE
1919-20	Mary teaches, high school science, Genoa, NE
1920, Sep. 22	Mary applies for Wyoming Teacher's Certificate
1920-21	Mary teaches, Moorcroft, WY
1921-22	Mary teaches, Ogallala, NE
1922	Mary returns to farm, Lincoln, NE
1923, April 23?	Ella Rhatigan Partington dies,Lincoln, NE
1926, July	Mary takes 3 graduate level courses, University of Nebraska, Lincoln, NE
1928	Mount St. Joseph's Academy is renamed Clarke College
1932	St. Patrick's school closed, due to lack of funds
1934	St. Patrick's Church school discontinued
1935, Sep. 20	Harold Partington writes his last will
1936	George VI coronation/Partington party
1939	St. Patrick's Church building auctioned and bought back by the church
1940's	Mary buys 8 to 10 goats

1942	St. Patrick's Church school reopened
1944, July 7	Harold Partington dies
1959, June	Sanitary Board moves to fill Partington Pond
1961, Oct. 25	10:20 p.m., Mary is shot by trespassers
1961, Oct. 26	Trespassers in yard
1961, Nov. 4	BBs shot through window
1961, Nov.(?)	Mary acquires gun
1961, Nov.(?)	Mary has telephone installed in house
1962, June 13	Man sleeping in car in front yard
1962, June 15	Mary interrupts couple having sex behind barn
1962, June 18	7 p.m., Mary robbed at gunpoint, tied up and blindfolded in her house
1962, June 19	5 a.m., intruder leaves, 7 a.m., Mary frees herself
1962, July 13	Mary shoots at trespassers
1963, Nov. 16	2 car loads of Southeast High School students caught trespassing
1964, Sep. 18	Mary shoots teenage girl vandalizing house
1965, Jan. 16	Arson. Grass ignited on porch during night
1965, Jan 17	Window shot out
1965, Jan. 20	3 bullets shot through window during night
1965, June 12	Trespassers throw rocks at house, caught
1966, Mar. 26	Trespassers in yard
1966, Mar. 31	Window shot out
1966, April 1	Stones thrown through window by 4 Southeast High School students
1966, April 2	2 bullets through east window, 1st floor
1966, April 4	Rocks through north window, 1st floor
1966, April 5-6	Sheriff report notes nothing happened
1966, April 8	Break in. Girl enters Mary's bedroom at night and steals flashlight. Caught.
1966, April 16	Vandals cut down tree and overturn outhouse
1966, July 10	2:25 a.m., 3 trespassers yelling from car
1966, Sep. 13	Harold Partington will filed, not for probate
1966, Oct. 25	10:10 p.m., trespassers in yard dump trash
1966, Oct. 26	3:12 a.m., Mary kills Earl Eldon Hill. Sheriff takes Mary's shotgun
1966, Nov. 23	10:30, 2 carloads of teenagers questioned by deputies in front of Mary's house
1966, Dec. 12	James Harold Partington dies
1967, Dec. 29	Shots fired at house
1968, Oct. 24	Obscene graffiti painted on house

1969, Aug. 7	Glass in front door shot out
1969, Nov. 9	Attempted burglary
1970, n.d.	Burglary
1970, n.d.	Malicious destruction of property
1970, n.d.	Rock thrown through window
1970, n.d.	Large group of boys gathered near house
1972, n.d.	Breaking and entering
1972, n.d.	Littering
1975	Mary's health failing, fainting spells
1976, n.d.	Breaking and entering
1976, n.d.	Vandalism
1976, Jan.	Mary moves to Ingerson "home" in Lincoln
1976	Mary breaks hip in fall, moved to Madonna Home, Lincoln, NE
1977, Mar.	House and property put up for sale, $175,000
1976, Jan. 18	Mary writes last will, Ingersons witness
1976, Aug. 12	Ella Grace Louise Partington (Kellogg) dies
1976, Dec.	Mary writes Partington family history
1977, n.d.	Demolition of house begins by Crawford Lumber
1977, June 23	Arson. House is burned
1977, July 19	Arson. Outbuilding burned & grass fires
1977(?)	House foundation and trees bulldozed
1979, June 12	Mary Ann Partington dies
1979, July 6	Mary's will filed with Lancaster County Court

Frances Grace Reinehr

Frances Grace Reinehr is the author of *Storyteaching (1984)*. Her articles have been published in *The Nebraska Humanist*, *Poetic Voices of America*, *The Augustan Age* and *The Executive Educator*. Reinehr, a North Dakota native, has taught in grade schools since 1967 when she earned an MS degree from the University of Nebraska-Lincoln. The recipient of the Nebraska Cooper Award for Excellence in Education in 1983 and 1986, Reinehr has been elected president of the Nebraska Council of Teachers of English two times.